CHRISTMAS EVE

by EDITH THACHER HURD

Pictures by CLEMENT HURD

HARPER & ROW, PUBLISHERS, New York and Evanston

For
SUSANNA

It was the raven who first knew about
the baby.
He was flying over Bethlehem when
suddenly the sky was full of angels.

It was the cock who first told the
world about it.
"Christus natus est."
"Christ is born," he crowed.

The curious duck in the barnyard heard the cock and quacked,

"Quando? Quando?" which means "When? When?"

She wanted to know when was the little baby born.

The raven, who had seen the angels, answered,

"Hac nocte. Hac nocte."

"This night. This night."

The ox lowed in his deep soft voice,

"Ubi? Ubi?"

"Where? Where?"

The lamb knew where and said,

"In Bethlehem. In Bethlehem."

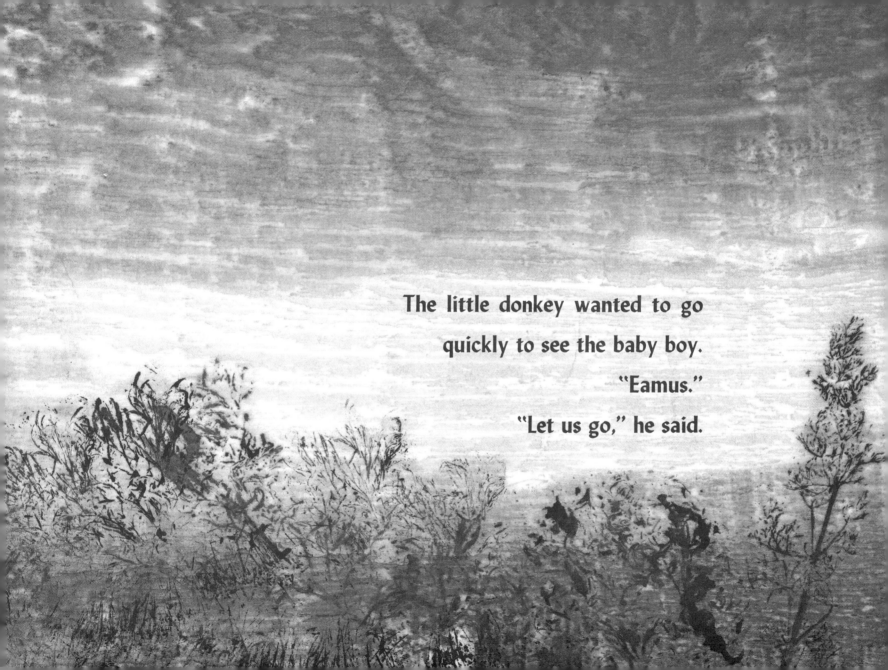

The little donkey wanted to go
quickly to see the baby boy.
"Eamus."
"Let us go," he said.

"Volo. Volo."
"I will. I will,"
the calf replied.

And so they went: the raven, the cock, the curious duck,
the ox, the lamb, the little donkey and the calf.
They all went to find the baby born in Bethlehem.

As they went a little bird flew with them.

It was the wren.

A beautiful deer joined them.

His antlers were like a great fir tree.

They walked in the cold night until
the little donkey and the calf were
tired, so they found a stable where
they could go in and rest.
They found the stable because a bright
star shone down on it.

The animals went in one by one.
But the deer, whose antlers were too
big, waited in the winter's night.

Inside, the animals found the little
baby boy.
He was sleeping in a manger.

The animals gathered around him

in the straw.

It was so cold in the stable

that the ox breathed his warm breath on him.

The wren brought soft moss and

gave her feathers to make a cover for him.

At twelve o'clock the animals knelt
down around the wooden manger.

Outside, the deer knelt too.

A white rose bloomed on a

rose tree beside the stable door.

Because it was this special night,
the animals could talk as people talk,
and they said,
"Welcome, little baby boy."

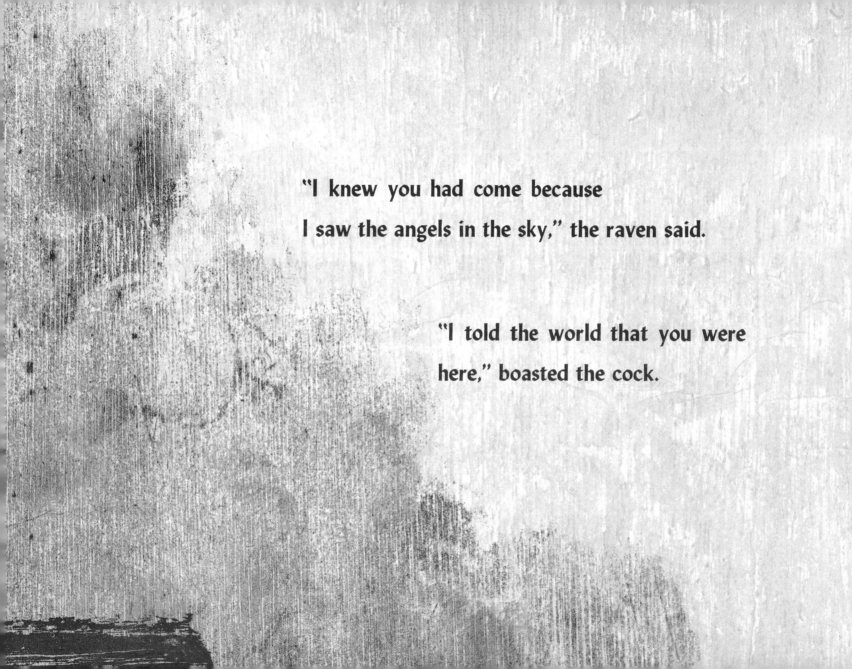

"I knew you had come because
I saw the angels in the sky," the raven said.

"I told the world that you were
here," boasted the cock.

"I knew it was in Bethlehem,"
the lamb said quietly.

"We have all come to see you,"
the little donkey said.

Outside, where the deer still
knelt, the birds sang all night long.
They sang more sweetly than they had
ever sung before.
The sparrows sang like nightingales.

In their hive the bees hummed a

Christmas Carol for the baby boy asleep.

Lullay, Thou little tiny Child.

By, by, lully, lullay.

Lullay, Thou little tiny Child.

By, by, lully, lullay.

Country people have long believed that on Christmas Eve barnyard animals are given the power to speak. Bees are known to hum a sweet carol in their hive on Christmas Eve. The deer, with spreading antlers, and the tiny wren are a part of Christmas lore in many lands. A white rose is said to have bloomed by the stable door. We still sing of this in the carol, "Lo, how a rose e'er blooming." It is from these simple beliefs and stories that this book has come.